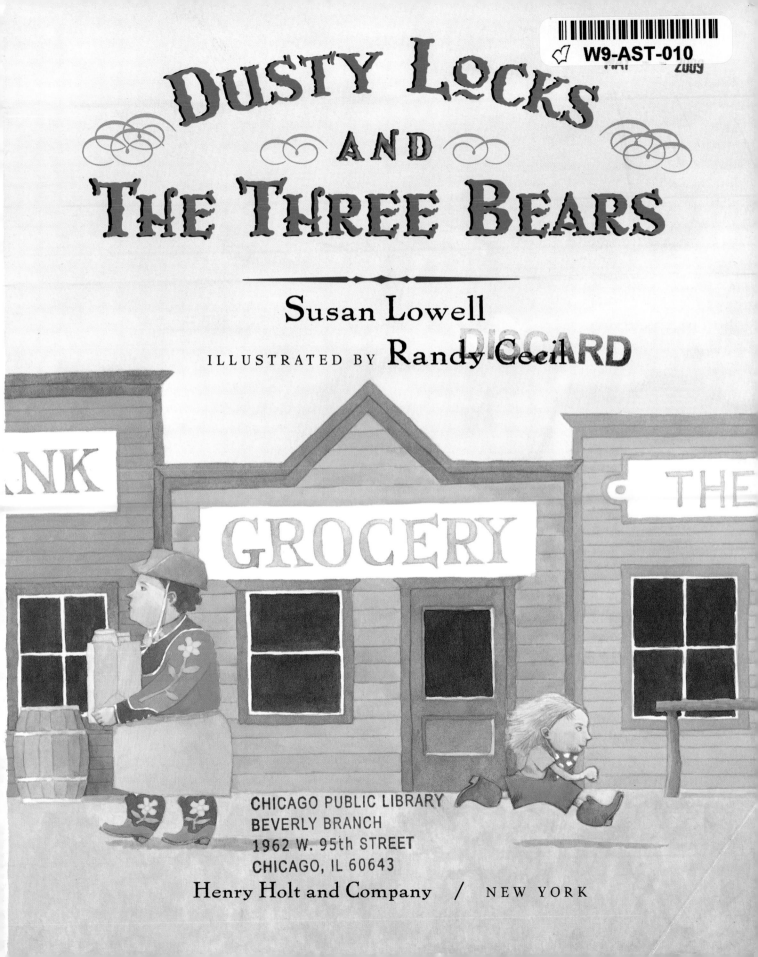

Dusty Locks

and

The Three Bears

Susan Lowell

ILLUSTRATED BY Randy Cecil

W9-AST-010

DISCARD

CHICAGO PUBLIC LIBRARY
BEVERLY BRANCH
1962 W. 95th STREET
CHICAGO, IL 60643

Henry Holt and Company / NEW YORK

Henry Holt and Company, LLC, *Publishers since 1866*
175 Fifth Avenue, New York, New York 10010
www.HenryHoltKids.com

Henry Holt® is a registered trademark of Henry Holt and Company, LLC .
Text copyright © 2001 by Susan Lowell
Illustrations copyright © 2001 by Randy Cecil
All rights reserved. Distributed in Canada by H. B. Fenn and Company Ltd.

Library of Congress Cataloging-in-Publication Data
Lowell, Susan. Dusty Locks and the three bears / Susan Lowell ; illustrations by Randy Cecil.
Summary : A Western-style retelling of the traditional tale about a little girl
who finds the house of a bear family and makes herself at home.
[1. Folklore.] I. Cecil, Randy, ill. II. Title.
PZ8.1.L9523Du 2001 398.2—dc21 [E] 00-28137

ISBN-13 : 978- 0-8050-5862-8 / ISBN-10 : 0-8050-5862-1 (hardcover)
7 9 10 8 6

ISBN-13 : 978- 0-8050-7534-2 / ISBN-10 : 0-8050-7534-8 (paperback)
3 5 7 9 10 8 6 4 2

First Hardcover Edition—2001 / First Paperback Edition—2004
The artist used acrylic gouache to create the illustrations for this book.
Designed by Martha Rago
Printed in China on acid-free paper. ∞

R0429807562

To Frances Kuffel,
who is just right
—S. L.

For Morgan
—R. C.

CHICAGO PUBLIC LIBRARY
BEVERLY BRANCH
1962 W. 95th STREET
CHICAGO, IL 60643

Once upon a time, way out West, there were three grizzly bears who lived together in a neat and tidy cabin in the woods.

One was a little bitty bear cub, just knee-high to a bumblebee. One was a mild-mannered middle-size mama. And one was a great big humpbacked gray-haired grizzly, nine feet tall and cross as two sticks.

They each had a dish to eat their beans from: a little
saucer for the bear cub, a tin plate for the mama bear, and a
great big turkey platter for the great big grizzly bear.

And they each had a seat to sit on: a three-legged stool for
the bear cub, a rocking chair for the mama bear, and a great
big lumpy stump for the great big grizzly bear.

And they each had a bed to sleep in: a little straw mattress for the bear cub,

a feather bed for the mama bear,

and a great big heap of prickly green branches for the great big grizzly bear.

One day, while their red-hot beans were cooling in their three dishes, the bears went out for a walk. And just as soon as they turned their grizzly backs, something strange came blowing out of the woods.

A cloud of smoke?

A swarm of mosquitoes?

No sirree! It was a dirty little girl.

She hadn't had a bath for a month of Sundays, so everybody called her Dusty Locks. But Trouble was her middle name. That little outlaw had run away from home without stopping to kiss her mother good-bye!

First Dusty Locks peeked in the bears' window. Then she squinted through the keyhole of the cabin door. Finally she barged right straight inside. Those grizzlies were fine, upstanding, law-abiding critters, honest as the day is long, and they never locked their door.

"Beans!" cried Dusty Locks. "Ya-hoo! I'm so hungry I could eat a saddle blanket."

Now, if the bears had been there, they would have shown true Western hospitality and said, "Sit right down and dig in!" But crusty little Dusty Locks didn't wait to be asked.

Next Dusty Locks sat on
the great big grizzly's stump.
"I'm rough and tough!"
she bragged.
But it was even too
lumpy and bumpy for *her*.

And then she tried the
mama bear's rocking chair,
but it had too many fancy-
dancy cushions for her. So
she plunked herself down
upon the bear cub's three-
legged stool.

"Just right!" said Dusty Locks.
But that heavy little roughneck sat the poor stool right into
the ground! This made her madder than a half-squashed hornet.
She kicked the pieces out of her way and stomped upstairs.

"Running away is hard
work," said Dusty Locks,
all tuckered out.

First she threw herself down on the heap of green
branches that belonged to the great big grizzly, but the
branches itched, and they pricked, and they jabbed, and
they stabbed Dusty Locks something terrible. So she
jumped up and down till she stamped them into sprigs.

Next she flopped onto the mama bear's feather bed.

"Ahh!" sighed Dusty Locks. "Mighty fine!"

But then she sank down deeper, and deeper, and
deeper, and . . .

"OOF!" cried Dusty Locks. "Too soft! Get me out
of here!"

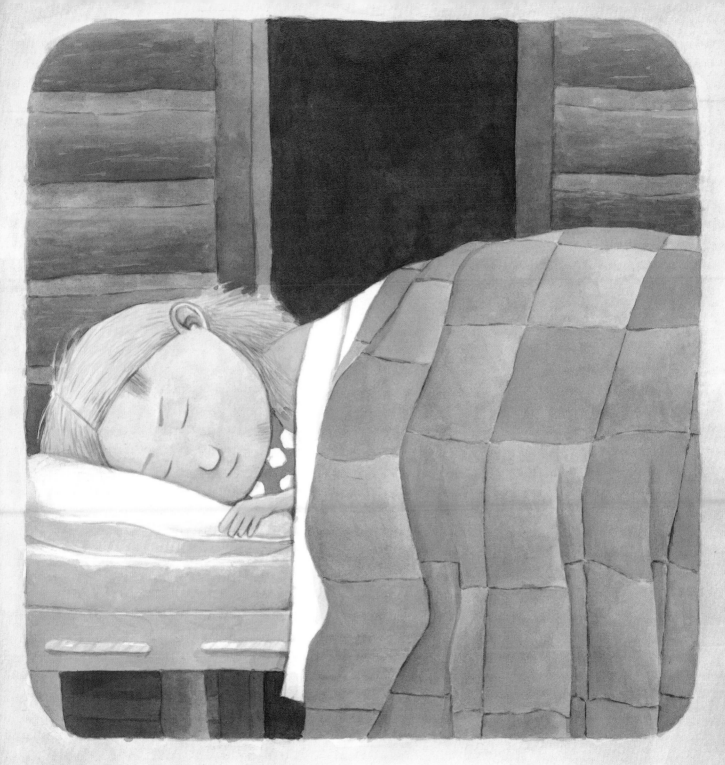

And then she tested the bear cub's little straw mattress, and it was neither too hard nor too soft.

"Just right!" said Dusty Locks, and she covered herself up and fell fast asleep.

Meanwhile the grizzlies came home from their hike. At first they figured their tidy cabin had been struck by a sandstorm. But when the great big grizzly took a look at his dinner, he got riled.

"SOMEONE'S BEEN EATING MY BEANS!" he growled in his great big rough gruff voice.

"Someone's been eating *my* beans!" said the mama bear in her mild-mannered middle-size voice.

"Someone's been eating *my* beans, too, *and has eaten them all up!*" squeaked the bear cub in his little bitty baby voice.

Now, Dusty Locks had tipped over the stump.

"SOMEONE'S BEEN SITTING IN MY CHAIR!" growled the big bear in his great big grouchy voice.

And Dusty Locks had dumped the cushions on the floor.

"Someone's been sitting in *my* chair!" said the mama bear in her middle-size voice.

"And someone's been sitting in *my* chair, *and smashed it all to flinders!*" squeaked the bear cub in a little bit bigger voice than before.

The great big grizzly got really riled.

"BEAN RUSTLER!" he roared. "CHAIR BUSTER!"

And the three bears galloped upstairs looking for trouble. The first thing they found was the heap of stomped sprigs.

"SOMEONE'S BEEN LYING IN MY BED!" growled the big bear in his great big gruesome voice.

Then they saw feathers scattered from here to breakfast.

"Someone's been lying in *my* bed!" said the mama bear in her middle voice.

And then they saw the little straw mattress, with a rumpled blanket and a dusty, dirty head upon the pillow.

"Someone's been lying in *my* bed, *and here she is!*" squeaked the bear cub in the biggest voice he had.

"WELL, I'LL BE BUMFUZZLED!" growled the great big bear, scratching his grizzly gray head in amazement.

"Land sakes!" said the mama bear. "Smells mighty whiffy in here!"

"Pee-YOO!" squeaked the bear cub. *"Is it a skunk?"*

When Dusty Locks heard the big grizzly's voice in her sleep, she dreamed of thunder and lightning. And when she heard the mama bear's voice, she dreamed of her own mother. But when she heard the bear cub's squeak, she dreamed she had a bug in her ear, and she woke right up.

And when she saw three grizzly bears staring at her, Dusty Locks was so scared that she tumbled out of bed, took a flying leap through the open window, and made tracks for home. She vamoosed so fast the dust didn't settle for a week.

The moment Dusty Locks's mother got ahold of that dirty little desperado, she dunked her in the bathtub, and then she scolded, and she scrubbed, and she rubbed, and she hugged, and she kissed Dusty Locks into a whole new girl entirely.

And the three grizzly bears never saw her again.

Or if they did . . . they never recognized her!